P9-CRJ-985

A Note to Parents and Caregivers:

Read-it! Readers are for children who are just starting on the amazing road to reading. These beautiful books support both the acquisition of reading skills and the love of books.

The RED LEVEL presents familiar topics using common words and repeating sentence patterns.
The BLUE LEVEL presents new ideas using a larger vocabulary and varied sentence structure.
The YELLOW LEVEL presents more challenging ideas, a broad vocabulary, and wide variety in sentence structure.

When sharing a book with your child, read in short stretches, pausing often to talk about the pictures. Have your child turn the pages and point to the pictures and familiar words. And be sure to reread favorite stories or parts of stories.

There is no right or wrong way to share books with children. Find time to read with your child and pass on the legacy of literacy.

Adria F. Klein, Ph.D.
Professor Emeritus
California State University
San Bernardino, California

First American edition published in 2003 by
Picture Window Books
5115 Excelsior Boulevard
Suite 232
Minneapolis, MN 55416
1-877-845-8392
www.picturewindowbooks.com

First published in Great Britain by Franklin Watts, 96 Leonard Street, London, EC2A 4XD
Text © Deborah Nash 2000
Illustration © Richard Morgan 2000

Printed in the United States of America.
1 2 3 4 5 6 08 07 06 05 04 03

Library of Congress Cataloging-in-Publication
Nash, Deborah.
   The Little Star / written by Deborah Nash ; illustrated by Richard Morgan.–1st American
ed.
     p. cm.—(Read-it! readers)
   Summary: When Little Star says he wants to live on the Earth, the Moon shows him how
much fun it is to live in the sky.
   ISBN 1-4048-0065-4
   [1. Stars—Fiction. 2. Moon—Fiction.] I. Morgan, Richard Charles, 1966-, ill. II. Title.
III. Series.
   PZ7.N1665 Li 2003
   [E]—dc21   2002074931

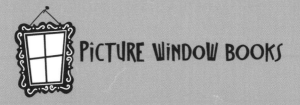

PiCTURE WiNDOW BOOKS

The Little Star

Written by Deborah Nash

Illustrated by Richard Morgan

Reading Advisors:
Adria F. Klein, Ph.D.
Professor Emeritus, California State University
San Bernardino, California

Ruth Thomas
Durham Public Schools
Durham, North Carolina

R. Ernice Bookout
Durham Public Schools
Durham, North Carolina

Picture Window Books
Minneapolis, Minnesota

Little Star looked down
from the sky.

"I want to live down there,"
said Little Star.

"You can't," said his mom. "That's Earth and you're a star."

Little Star was very sad.

He went to visit the Moon.

"It's fun living in the sky,"
said the Moon.

"Come with me. I can show you."

Little Star and the Moon
zoomed around the
Milky Way.

They bounced up and down on soft, fluffy clouds.

They cooked hot dogs
by the heat of the Sun.

They slid down a rainbow.

18

They played soccer
with the planets.

"The sky is not so bad,
after all," said Little Star.

"In fact, I think I like it!"

Little Star's mom and dad
were glad he wanted to stay.

25

Little Star flew high up
into the sky.

Down on Earth, people
saw him shoot by.

"What's that up there?"
a little boy asked.

"It's a shooting star,"
said his dad.

"I want to live up there,"
said the little boy.

"You can't," said his dad.
"You're a boy, not a star!"

Red Level

The Best Snowman, by Margaret Nash 1-4048-0048-4
Bill's Baggy Pants, by Susan Gates 1-4048-0050-6
Cleo and Leo, by Anne Cassidy 1-4048-0049-2
Felix on the Move, by Maeve Friel 1-4048-0055-7
Jasper and Jess, by Anne Cassidy 1-4048-0061-1
The Lazy Scarecrow, by Jillian Powell 1-4048-0062-X
Little Joe's Big Race, by Andy Blackford 1-4048-0063-8
The Little Star, by Deborah Nash 1-4048-0065-4
The Naughty Puppy, by Jillian Powell 1-4048-0067-0
Selfish Sophie, by Damian Kelleher 1-4048-0069-7

Blue Level

The Bossy Rooster, by Margaret Nash 1-4048-0051-4
Jack's Party, by Ann Bryant 1-4048-0060-3
Little Red Riding Hood, by Maggie Moore 1-4048-0064-6
Recycled!, by Jillian Powell 1-4048-0068-9
The Sassy Monkey, by Anne Cassidy 1-4048-0058-1
The Three Little Pigs, by Maggie Moore 1-4048-0071-9

Yellow Level

Cinderella, by Barrie Wade 1-4048-0052-2
The Crying Princess, by Anne Cassidy 1-4048-0053-0
Eight Enormous Elephants, by Penny Dolan 1-4048-0054-9
Freddie's Fears, by Hilary Robinson 1-4048-0056-5
Goldilocks and the Three Bears, by Barrie Wade 1-4048-0057-3
Mary and the Fairy, by Penny Dolan 1-4048-0066-2
Jack and the Beanstalk, by Maggie Moore 1-4048-0059-X
The Three Billy Goats Gruff, by Barrie Wade 1-4048-0070-0